The Magic Footprints

Melissa Balfour * Russell Julian

Green Bananas

Crabtree Publishing Company
www.crabtreebooks.com

PMB 16A, 350 Fifth Avenue,
Suite 3308,
New York, NY 10118

616 Welland Avenue,
St. Catharines, Ontario
Canada, L2M 5V6

Balfour, Melissa.
  The magic footprints / written by Melissa Balfour ; illustrated by Russell
Julian.
      p. cm. -- (Green bananas)
  Summary: When the new girl next door gives Tim, who is very shy, a
mysterious birthday present, the two children become friends.
  ISBN-13: 978-0-7787-1023-3 (reinforced lib. bdg. : alk. paper)
  ISBN-10: 0-7787-1023-8 (reinforced lib. bdg. : alk. paper)
  ISBN-13: 978-0-7787-1039-4 (pbk. : alk. paper)
  ISBN-10: 0-7787-1039-4 (pbk. : alk. paper)
  [1. Friendship--Fiction. 2. Gifts--Fiction.] I. Julian, Russell, 1975-
ill. II. Title. III. Series.
  PZ7.B197575Mag 2005
  [E]--dc22

2005001572
LC

Published by Crabtree Publishing in 2005
First published in 2005 by Egmont Books Ltd.
Text copyright © Melissa Balfour 2005
Illustrations copyright © Russell Julian 2005
The Author and Illustrator have asserted their moral rights.
Paperback ISBN 0-7787-1039-4
Reinforced Hardcover Binding ISBN 0-7787-1023-8

**Tim's
Birthday**

**Lola's
Present**

Surprise!

For Gabriel,
love Mummy.

For Phillip and Glenys Julian,
my mum and dad,
R.J.

Tim's Birthday

It was Tim's birthday. Wig and Zip
gave him a perfect blue plane.

They put on party hats. Tim played
with his plane.

He blew out all the candles on his cake.

Somebody was watching Tim and

Wig and Zip. Somebody new.

Wheeeee!

Tim played with his plane.

It did loop the loops.

Tim dropped his plane.

Somebody laughed.

"Hello," said Somebody.

Tim's plane flew behind a chair.

"I'm Lola," said Lola.

Tim's plane flew behind a tree.

Tim's plane peeped out. Then Tim

peeped out. Lola had gone.

The doorbell rang.

It was Lola. "Happy Birthday!"

"Goodbye, Lola."

Lola's Present

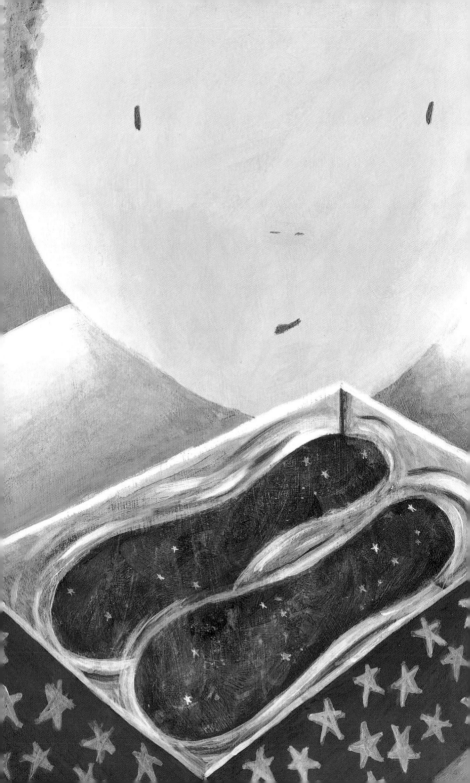

Tim opened his present.

Lola had given him footprints.

Tim left them in the box. He played with his plane.

Tim liked his plane best.

ee-ow!

It could fly up in the sky . . .

really high . . .

turn upside down . . .

and land on the water.

It was bedtime.

Wig put the footprints in Zip's cage.

Tim noticed his footprints.

He was surprised.

Tim opened the cage door.

Then he got into bed.

Surprise!

During the night, Tim woke up.

His footprints were gone.

He looked out of the window.

They were in the garden!

Tim went into the night.

He followed his footprints . . .

and found Lola!

Tim's footprints flew out of his hands.

They flew up in the sky . . .

. . . and into Lola's garden.

There
they are.

Lola and Tim followed them.

They climbed over the fence.

The footprints were flying over

the pond.

They floated down and went splash.

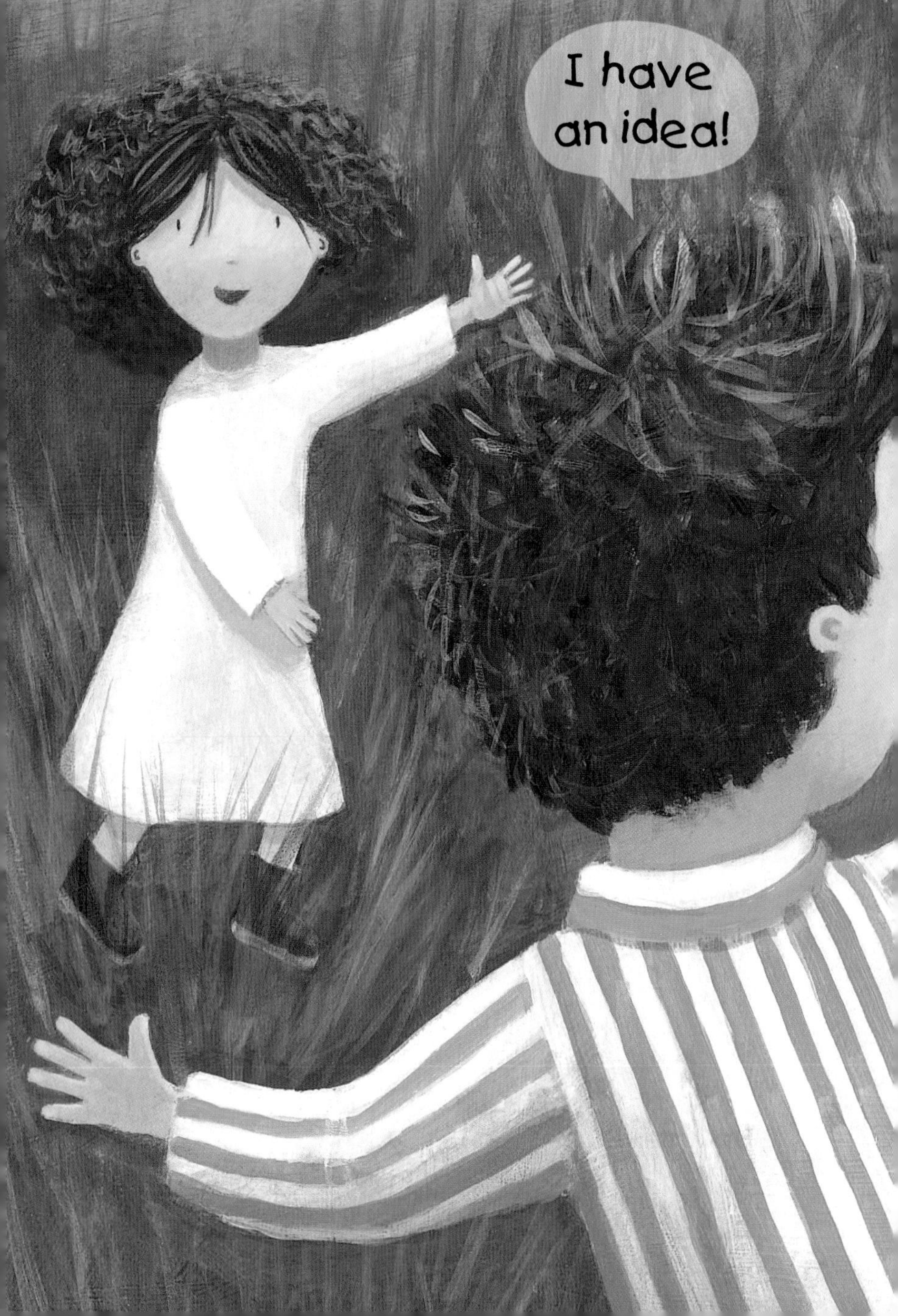

Lola and Tim looked in the pond.

The footprints were jumping.

Zip caught one in his beak.

Tim went fishing for footprints.

Look!

Wig barked. A light had gone on
in Lola's house.

Goodnight, Lola.

Goodnight, Tim.